The Child's World®

Published by The Child's World®
1980 Lookout Drive • Mankato, MN 56003-1705
800-599-READ • www.childsworld.com

ACKNOWLEDGMENTS
The Child's World®: Mary Berendes, Publishing Director
The Design Lab: Kathleen Petelinsek, Design and Page Production
Literacy Consultants: Cecilia Minden, PhD, and Joanne Meier, PhD

LIBRARY OF CONGRESS
CATALOGING-IN-PUBLICATION DATA
Moncure, Jane Belk.
  My "l" sound box / by Jane Belk Moncure ;
illustrated by Rebecca Thornburgh.
    p. cm. — (Sound box books)
  Summary: "Little l has an adventure with items beginning with
his letter's sound, such as lizards, a little lion, and a lighthouse by
the lake."—Provided by publisher.
  ISBN 978-1-60253-152-9 (library bound : alk. paper)
  [1. Alphabet.] I. Thornburgh, Rebecca McKillip, ill. II. Title.
PZ7.M739Myl 2009
[E]—dc22   2008033168

Printed in the United States of America • Mankato, MN
August, 2011 • PA02105

A NOTE TO PARENTS AND EDUCATORS:

Magic moon machines and five fat frogs are just a few of the fun things you can share with children by reading books with them. Reading aloud helps children in so many ways! It introduces them to new words, motivates them to develop their own reading skills, and expands their attention span and listening abilities. So it's important to find time each day to share a book or two . . . or three!

As you read with young children, you can help develop their understanding of how print works by talking about the parts of the book—the cover, the title, the illustrations, and the words that tell the story. As you read, use your finger to point to each word, modeling a gentle sweep from left to right.

Simple word games help develop important prereading skills, including an understanding of rhyme and alliteration (when words share the same beginning sound, such as "six" and "sand"). Try playing with words from a book you've just shared: "What other words start with the same sound as moon?" "Cat and hat, do those words rhyme?" The possibilities are endless—and so are the rewards!

My "I" Sound Box®

WRITTEN BY JANE BELK MONCURE

ILLUSTRATED BY REBECCA THORNBURGH

Little  had a box. "I will find things that begin with my **I** sound," he said. "I will put them into my sound box."

Little  looked under some leaves and found lizards. Did he put the leaves and the lizards into his box? He did.

Then Little  looked behind some logs and found lambs.

They were little lambs.

"You must be lost," said Little .

So he put the little lambs and the logs into the box with the leaves and the lizards.

Then Little  walked to a lake.

The lizards leaped out of the box.

But Little I put them back.

"I do not like leaping lizards,"

he said.

Little  looked in the lake and found a lobster.

He lifted the lobster into the box

. . . carefully . . . because the

lobster had long claws.

Then Little  saw a lighthouse by the lake.

He went inside the lighthouse.

The lantern was not on. So

Little 🧒 climbed up the

ladder . . .

. . . and lit the lantern.

"Someone might be lost,"

he said.

Little 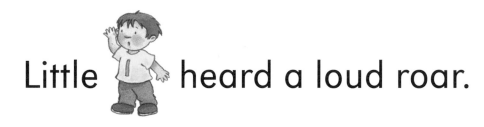 heard a loud roar.

He opened the door and found a little lion.

The little lion licked him.

The little lion sat in his lap.

He gave the lion a lollipop.

"You must be lost," he said.

"You belong in my sound box."

Little  heard another loud roar.

He opened the door and found a
little leopard.

The little leopard licked him.

The little leopard sat in his lap.

Little  gave the leopard a lollipop.

"You must be lost," he said.

"You belong in my sound box."

But when he put the little  leopard into the box . . .

. . . the lobster pinched the leopard's

leg. The leopard leaped. The lion

leaped. The lambs and lizards

leaped, too.

So Little  put the lobster into a lobster pot.

Just then, he heard another loud

roar. He opened the door and

saw a locomotive.

"Let's go for a long ride!" he said.

Little l's Word List

ladder 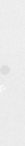	leaves 	lizard 
lake 	leg 	lobster 
lamb	leopard	locomotive 
lantern	lighthouse 	log
lap 	lion 	lollipop 

Other Words with Little l

lace

lady

ladybug

lamp

lasso

laundry

lemons

letter

lettuce

light

lily

lips

lock

locket

lunch box

More to Do!

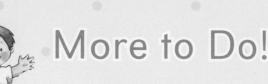

Little had a good time with all the animals!
He wrote to his friend, Lily, about his adventures.

Dear Lily,

Today I looked in some leaves and logs. I found lizards and lambs! The lizards kept leaping out of my box. I do not like leaping lizards.

Next I went to the lake and saw a lighthouse. Can you guess what I found when I went inside? I found a little lion and a leopard. I gave each of them a lollipop.

We all took a ride on a locomotive. It was a very fun day.

Love,
Little l

Lisa Llama
125 Lollipop Lane
LaLoon, LA
12345

Try It!

You can write to someone you love, too. Write about what you did today. You can tell the person that you read a book about the sound of **l**!

About the Author

Best-selling author Jane Belk Moncure has written over 300 books throughout her teaching and writing career. After earning a Master's degree in Early Childhood Education from Columbia University, she became one of the pioneers in that field. In 1956, she helped form the Virginia Association for Early Childhood Education, which established the first statewide standards for teachers of young children.

Inspired by her work in the classroom, Mrs. Moncure's books have become standards in primary education, and her name is recognized across the country. Her success is reflected not only in her books' popularity with parents, children, and educators, but also by numerous awards, including the 1984 C. S. Lewis Gold Medal Award.

About the Illustrator

Rebecca Thornburgh lives in a pleasantly spooky old house in Philadelphia. If she's not at her drawing table, she's reading—or singing with her band, called Reckless Amateurs. Rebecca has one husband, two daughters, and two silly dogs.